Special thanks to Linda Chapman

To Holly Vitow – super efficient,
super hard working, super tolerant
and incredibly sparkly.
Thank you!

ORCHARD BOOKS
338 Euston Road, London NW1 3BH
Orchard Books Australia
Level 17/207 Kent Street, Sydney, NSW 2000
A Paperback Original

First published in 2013 by Orchard Books

Text © Hothouse Fiction Limited 2013

Illustrations © Orchard Books 2013

A CIP catalogue record for this book is available
from the British Library.

ISBN 978 1 408 32376 2

1 3 5 7 9 10 8 6 4 2

Printed in Great Britain

The paper and board used in this paperback are natural recyclable
products made from wood grown in sustainable forests. The
manufacturing processes conform to the environmental regulations
of the country of origin.

Orchard Books is a division of Hachette Children's Books,
an Hachette UK company

www.hachette.co.uk

Series created by Hothouse Fiction

www.hothousefiction.com

Reading Consultant: Prue Goodwin,
lecturer in literacy and children's books

Bubble Volcano

ROSIE BANKS

ORCHARD

The Secret Kingdom

Bubble Volcano

Contents

A Special Invitation

"Summer, come on!" Jasmine Smith urged. "Ellie will be wondering where we are!"

"Just a minute!" Summer Hammond was crouched on the ground, her blonde pigtails falling over her shoulders as she coaxed a tiny red ladybird off the pavement and onto her hand. She gently placed it down on a nearby wall. "It'll be safe there," she said to Jasmine. "I couldn't leave it. Someone might have trodden on it."

Jasmine smiled. Summer loved all animals, even insects like ladybirds. "When you're older, you'll have to get a job on one of those TV animal shows where they film at a zoo or a vet's office."

Summer looked horrified. "Oh, no. I'd hate to be on TV."

"I'd love it!" said Jasmine. She flung her arms out and twirled round. Her long dark hair flew around her shoulders as she spun. "Imagine being an actress, or even better, a pop star!"

Summer grinned. She and Jasmine and their other best friend, Ellie Macdonald, were all very different from one another, but maybe that was why they all got on so well — that, and the fact they shared an amazing magical secret, of course! Summer felt a tingle of excitement run through her as she thought about the precious object inside her bag.

"Come on, slowcoach!" she teased Jasmine. "I'll race you to Ellie's!"

"You're here!" Ellie squealed, flinging open the door as Jasmine and Summer ran up the drive, panting and out of breath. The three girls hugged. Ellie had been on holiday for two whole weeks. Her usually pale skin was covered with freckles from the sun and her red curls were slightly lighter than normal. "Come in!" she cried as she dragged Jasmine and Summer inside.

"Hi, girls!" Mrs Macdonald called from the kitchen.

Jasmine and Summer chorused hello.

"We're going upstairs, Mum!" Ellie said.

The girls bounded up the stairs to Ellie's

bedroom. Jasmine looked around at the purple walls, which were covered with pictures that Ellie had drawn herself. It felt like ages since she had last been here – two weeks was a long time to be apart from one of your best friends!

"Ta-da!" Ellie cried as she picked two little presents up off the desk and held them out to Jasmine and Summer. They were wrapped in paper she had decorated herself. She had drawn rabbits on Summer's and musical notes on Jasmine's. "These are for you. I bought them in Spain."

"Oh, thank you!" Jasmine and Summer exclaimed, quickly unwrapping the gifts. Inside Jasmine's was a small model of a dark-haired flamenco dancer wearing a red silk dress and inside Summer's there was a toy donkey with long ears and a very cute face.

"Thanks, Ellie!" Jasmine smiled. "I love it!"

"My donkey's so sweet!" said Summer, stroking its furry head.

Ellie beamed. "I'm glad you like them."

She lowered her voice. "So, what's been going on here while I've been away? You didn't go *you-know-where* without me, did you?" she asked anxiously.

"No!" Jasmine grinned. "We haven't had any messages in the *you-know-what*."

"You mean this *you-know-what*?" Summer asked, pulling a wooden box out of her bag.

"The Magic Box!" breathed Ellie.

Summer put it down on the rug gently. It had mermaids, unicorns and other wonderful creatures carved into its sides, and in the middle of its lid there was a mirror surrounded by six green gems.

The Magic Box came from a place called the Secret Kingdom. King Merry, the ruler there, had made it to help save the kingdom. When he was chosen to lead instead of his nasty sister, Queen Malice, the evil queen had hidden six horrible thunderbolts around the Secret

Kingdom to cause problems and ruin everyone's fun. The Magic Box had travelled to the human world and found the only people who could break Queen Malice's awful spells – Summer, Jasmine and Ellie!

With the help of King Merry's pixie assistant, Trixi, and lots of wonderful friends from the Secret Kingdom, the girls had broken all six of Malice's thunderbolts and helped the enchanted land return to peace and happiness. Queen Malice had sworn that she would find another way to rule the Secret Kingdom, but so far there were no more signs of trouble.

"It's been ages since we got any messages in the Magic Box," said Jasmine. "Nothing's happened for *months!*"

"That's probably good – for the Secret
Kingdom, anyway," pointed out Summer.
"It must mean everything is fine there."

Jasmine sighed. "I don't want anything
bad to happen in the Secret Kingdom,
but I really wish we could visit again!"

"Or at least open the Magic Box," Ellie
said. "If we could see all the amazing
gifts we've been given, then it wouldn't
feel as if we dreamed it all!"

Inside the box there were six tiny
compartments, each containing a
magical item that the girls had been
given on one of their adventures. There
was a map of the Secret Kingdom, a
tiny silver unicorn horn that let them
talk to animals, a crystal that controlled
the weather, an icy hourglass that could
freeze time, a pearl that made them

invisible and a tiny bag of glitter dust with enough of the magical powder in it to grant them each one wish. It would have been lovely to take the things out and look at them, but the girls knew that the box only opened when the gifts were needed.

Ellie looked at their reflection in the mirrored lid and sighed. "I really do miss King Merry and Trixi…"

"I'd love to see the unicorns again," Summer said.

"And all the mermaids and brownies and imps," added Jasminc.

Ellie shivered. "But not Queen Malice. I *definitely* wouldn't want to see her!"

"Do you remember when she tried to destroy Cloud Island?" said Jasmine.

Summer nodded. "And how she tried to

ruin the Golden Games for the unicorns and—" She broke off with a gasp as the mirror on the lid of the Magic Box began to shine. "Look! The box!"

They all stared as words started to form on the surface. "That's funny," Ellie said.

"What?" asked Summer, peering over her shoulder with Jasmine. "Oh, I see what you mean! This riddle sounds like it's from Trixi!" She grinned as she thought about the beautiful royal pixie who looked after King Merry.

Ellie read it out, her voice shaking with excitement:

"Human friends, please hear my call,
And join us at a springtime ball.
Think of the place King Merry likes best,
And pixie magic will do the rest."

"So we have to think of King Merry's favourite place," said Jasmine, sitting back on her heels. "Hmmm…"

"Easy," Summer said immediately. "His palace!"

They all knew what to do next. They put their hands on the green gems and called out: "The answer is the Enchanted Palace!"

The box flew open and a beam of silvery light exploded out. It hit the ceiling and suddenly there in the circle of light was a small pixie standing on top of a floating leaf. Her messy blonde hair had pretty flowers in it, and her blue eyes sparkled under the jewelled tiara perched on her head. She was wearing a pink ball gown with a sweeping skirt covered in tiny white pearls and golden dancing shoes with pink ribbon ties that matched her dress.

"Trixibelle!" exclaimed Ellie in delight.

"Ellie, Summer, Jasmine!" the pixie cried, flying her leaf down to kiss them all on the tips of their noses. "It's lovely to see you again! I'm so happy you got my message."

"We are, too!" Jasmine said. "But why

didn't the Magic Box
send us a riddle
like it normally
does?"

The little
pixie hovered
over the box
and tapped it
with her tiny
finger. "Now
that you've
saved the Secret
Kingdom and the box
is full, its job is done! But as long as you
have it, I'll be able to use it to send you
messages."

"Great!" said Jasmine.

"Have you really come to take us to a
ball?" asked Summer.

"Yes!" Trixi beamed. "We usually only have a ball once a year – on the first day of summer – but this year we have something to celebrate, so we're going to have two!"

"Wow!" said Ellie excitedly. "What are you celebrating?"

"Queen Malice hasn't done anything nasty since you broke all of her thunderbolts," Trixi explained, "and King Merry is so happy that he decided to invite everyone to the Enchanted Palace for a spring ball. I'm in charge of organising it all. You girls helped us so much that we couldn't possibly have it without you there!" She did a little twirl on her leaf. "So what do you say? Would you like to come to the most magical party ever?"

"Oh, yes!" Ellie, Summer and Jasmine all cried, jumping to their feet.

"Then hold hands." Trixi grinned. "And you *shall* go to the ball!"

The Springtime Ball

Ellie, Summer and Jasmine held hands while Trixi tapped her magic pixie ring and chanted:

> "Pixie magic, please take us all
> To the palace for the ball!"

As Trixi spoke, her words appeared in the mirror on the Magic Box. They glowed there for an instant and then streamed upwards in a blaze of purple

light and whirled around the girls' heads
in a glittering cloud. Jasmine, Summer
and Ellie squeezed one another's hands
tightly as they felt their feet leaving the
ground.

The whirlwind swirled them away
and they landed on something soft,
surrounded by a cloud of purple glitter.
As the air cleared, the girls looked
around. They were sitting on a comfy
sofa in an enormous room with deep
peacock-blue walls and a high domed
ceiling. There were big windows looking
out over beautiful gardens, and gleaming
chandeliers hung down from the roof,
sparkling with light. At one end of the
hall a band of brownies were setting
up their musical instruments and at the
other end a group of fairies were flying

along the walls, hanging up long lines of pretty twinkle-twinkle bunting. Elf butlers bustled about between carrying plates of delicious-looking food and placing them on long tables.

"We've never been in this part of the Enchanted Palace," said Summer. "Where are we?"

"This is the palace ballroom," Trixi said, spinning round in the air on her leaf.

"It's beautiful!" said Jasmine. She didn't know what to look at first. As she glanced round the room she caught sight of their reflection in one of the huge gold-framed mirrors on the wall. With a smile, she saw that the tiaras that King Merry had given her, Summer and Jasmine to show that they were his special helpers had magically appeared

on their heads. They were the perfect
things to wear at a royal ball!

Suddenly the main ballroom doors
flew open and King Merry entered. His
cheeks were a rosy red and white curls
poked out from under his shining crown.
He was wearing a smart purple velvet
cloak with tiny crowns embroidered all
over it in golden thread. There were real
gemstones sewn around the edges of the
robe, and they sparkled in the light of
the chandeliers as he walked towards
the girls. "Ah, my friends from the Other
Realm!" he cried delightedly. "How
wonderful to see you again!" He hurried
over to them, his eyes twinkling behind
his half-moon spectacles.

All three girls curtsied.

"Now, now, there's no need for that,"

King Merry told them fondly. "You are
my honoured guests. After all, if you
hadn't stopped my horrible sister then
we wouldn't be having this party!" He
turned to Trixi. "Is everything ready for
the big celebration?"

"Yes, King Merry," answered Trixi,
smoothing down her glittery dress. "The
guests will be arriving any minute."

"Excellent!" King Merry looked around
happily. "The food looks delicious. The
elves have done a wonderful job."

"Everything looks amazing!" Ellie
agreed.

"There are so many delicious-looking
things I've never seen before," said
Jasmine. "I can't wait to try them!"

"I'd thoroughly recommend the
rainbow jellies," King Merry advised her,

motioning to the towers
of stripy jellies that
were almost as tall as
the girls.

"Or the frosted
cherries," Trixi said,
pointing at a silver bowl
full of red cherries covered with a white
sugar coating. "They're my favourite!"

"Frosted cherries?" A look of concern
crossed King Merry's face. "But Trixi, you
know what happened last time we had
frosted cherries…" His glasses wobbled
on his nose in alarm.

"What happened?" Summer asked,
patting the king's arm kindly.

"We had frosted cherries once when
King Merry was giving a dinner for a
party of pixies," Trixi explained. "But

some stink toads had hidden in with them and when we opened the cherries the stink toads hopped out and ruined everything! They ate all the food, chased the pixies and left a horrible smell *everywhere*. It took days to get rid of them all. They love making things smelly and awful, and they really hate us pixies because we like to make people happy."

Jasmine shivered. "They sound terrible. Even you couldn't like a stink toad, Summer."

"Probably not," Summer admitted. She didn't think she could like anything that hated pixies.

"But don't worry, Your Majesty," Trixi said soothingly. "The elves checked the frosted cherries before they brought them in. There are no stink toads anywhere around."

"Good, good!" King Merry smiled.
Suddenly the trumpeters by the door
started to play a loud fanfare. "The guests
are arriving!" he cried happily, tripping
over his cloak in excitement.

Jasmine, Summer and Ellie hastily
helped him up while Trixi straightened
his crown.

"Oh, thank you," King Merry said.
"Now I'm ready for a party! Let the
spring ball begin!"

Soon the hall was filled with hundreds
of guests. The fairies fluttered between
the shining lights of the chandeliers, the
brownie band played lively music and the
imps danced merrily.

Jasmine, Summer and Ellie sat down on
one side of King Merry's throne at the

long head table, and Trixi sat on his other side, in a pixie-sized chair set up on the table. The elf butlers brought huge plates of food to the table and the girls were surprised to see that the first course was pudding!

"I always start with dessert because it's my favourite," King Merry laughed. "This way I don't have to wait for it!"

Jasmine decided to have a delicious-looking rainbow jelly, and Summer took a giant iced cookie that was decorated with sugar unicorns. Ellie started with frosted cherries and trifle.

King Merry's eyes lit up as a tall elf wearing a hood placed a big fluffy cake in front of him. "Ooh, a marshmallow cake! Yummy!"

"I don't remember ordering any marshmallow cakes…" Trixi said, her forehead crinkling. "Oh, well. I guess someone else must have thought of it. Enjoy it, King Merry!"

"I will!" The king plunged his spoon into the sticky sweet cake and took a big mouthful.

CRACK!!!

Instantly there was a loud thunderclap and a flash of lightning. Everyone screamed and the girls grabbed one another's hands.

"What's happening?" King Merry asked nervously.

"I don't know," said Trixi. "I—"

Her voice was drowned out by the sound of cackling laughter. Silence fell across the ballroom as the elf who had put the cake in front of the king drew back his hood. It wasn't an elf after all, but a tall, thin woman with cold dark eyes and a spiky crown perched on top of her frizzy black hair.

"Queen Malice!" Jasmine gasped.

The Evil Spell

"Oh, no!" breathed Summer, squeezing Ellie and Jasmine's hands tightly.

"You have fallen into my trap, brother!" Queen Malice cackled as the crowd fell back, leaving her standing on her own. She pointed at King Merry with a bony finger. "And now you are going to be very, very sorry!"

"What trap?" King Merry asked

indignantly. "Why are you here, Malice?
I suppose you've come to spoil everyone's
fun, as always!"

"I've come to do much more than
that, dear brother," the queen gloated.
She pointed at the marshmallow cake.
"I knew you'd be too greedy to resist a
marshmallow cake, so I made one and
poisoned it with a curse – one mouthful
is enough to turn whoever eats it into a
stink toad!"

"No!" cried Trixi.

Jasmine, Ellie and Summer gasped in
horror.

"A…a stink toad!" King Merry
stammered. "I'm going to be…a *stink
toad*?"

"Yes!" Queen Malice's icy eyes glinted
in delight. "The magic is starting to

transform you even as we speak. It will be complete by midnight on the day of the summer ball, and then I will rule the kingdom!" Queen Malice looked round the room, smiling cruelly at everyone's shocked faces. "Don't worry, dear brother," she continued. "There will always be a place for you here at the palace – *in the moat!*"

She threw back her head and shrieked with delight as all the guests started to cry out in protest. "I said you'd be sorry for stopping my thunderbolts, Merry. Now I'll finally get back at you, and those pesky human friends of yours. I'm going to rule this kingdom my way, and there will be no more balls, no more parties – and *no more FUN!*"

Queen Malice laughed gleefully and

clapped her hands. There was another deafening crack and then she vanished in a puff of black smoke.

"What are we going to do?" cried Trixi in despair.

"I can't be a stink toad!" King Merry exclaimed, wringing his hands. "I can't!"

"Don't worry," said Jasmine fiercely. "We'll help. We've broken Queen Malice's spells before, and we can do it again."

"Of course we can," declared Ellie and Summer.

"Oh, thank you…*RRRIBBIT*!"

Trixi and the girls gasped as the king let out a loud croaking noise.

King Merry grew pale. "I'm…I'm turning into a stink toad already!" he cried, staggering backwards and sinking onto his throne.

Jasmine turned to Trixi. "Can you use magic to stop Queen Malice's curse?"

Trixi shook her head anxiously. "My magic's not strong enough!"

"But there are loads of magical creatures here," said Ellie thoughtfully. "What if everyone worked together like we did at Glitter Beach?"

"Hmmm..." Trixi thought. "Our magic was stronger then because we'd just absorbed the glitter dust. But it's worth a try!" Trixi zipped away to speak to the others. Within a few minutes everyone had gathered around the king in a circle.

"What's going on?" King Merry asked Trixi.

"Don't worry, Your Majesty," Trixi replied. "We're going to try and make

you better!" Trixi tapped her ring and
called out:

"Pixie magic, stop the spell,
Make King Merry strong and well."

All the other creatures joined hands
around the circle and repeated the chant
along with Trixi.

"Do you feel any different?" Summer
asked King Merry hopefully.

"Maybe." King Merry waggled his

arms and legs. "It might have worked. It...*RRRIBBIT!*"

Everyone groaned.

"It's not working!" King Merry cried, his eyes filling with tears. He walked over to his throne and slumped down in it sadly.

"If our magic can't undo it," said Trixi in despair, "there isn't anything we can do."

"There must be something!" Jasmine said determinedly. "If he was poisoned by eating one thing, isn't there something else he can eat to undo it?"

"Actually, yes there is," said a calm voice. They turned and saw an older pixie flying through the crowd on a leaf. Her hair was in a neat bun, and she had glasses perched on her tiny pixie nose.

"Aunt Maybelle!"
Trixi said, giving
her a big hug.
"Girls, this is my
aunt. She's on
the pixie council.
She knows
everything there
is to know about
magic!"

"Pixie magic can't undo the queen's
wicked curse," Maybelle said grimly. "But
there is a counter-potion King Merry can
drink that should reverse it. It's our only
hope."

Jasmine's eyes lit up. "Perfect! How do
we make it?"

"Well, that's the problem," Maybelle
said unhappily. "It requires six very rare

ingredients from all around the Secret Kingdom."

"We'll get them for you," Ellie said quickly.

"Of course we will!" Summer cried.

"It will be very difficult – and *dangerous*," Maybelle warned.

"It doesn't matter," insisted Jasmine. "We have to try. We can't let Queen Malice turn King Merry into a stink toad! We'll go and get everything you need."

Summer and Ellie nodded bravely.

"But what about the others?" Summer said, looking round at all the upset guests. The pixies were crying into large hankies, the brownies were huddled together talking anxiously and the elves were shouting and waving their arms.

"Everyone looks so worried! Is there anything we can do to help them?"

"What we need is a strong forgetting spell," Maybelle said. "It will be better if the others forget everything so they don't panic." She looked over at Trixi. "Will you help with the spell?" she asked. "We're not fighting Queen Malice's magic, so it should work this time."

Trixi nodded. "We'll make it so only the five of us know what's happened, and no one else will remember."

Trixi and Maybelle tapped their rings and chanted:

"Pixie magic, banish their fear,
So they forget what's happened here."

Clouds of pink sparkles burst out

of their rings and
changed into
glittering
confetti. The
guests pointed
and gasped
as it floated
down from
the ceiling.

"Look what's
happening!"
gasped Jasmine.

Every time a piece of confetti landed
on a guest, the anxiety faded from
their face and they blinked and looked
surprised as if they couldn't quite
remember what they'd been worrying
about.

"The spell's working!" cried Ellie.

The girls watched as the brownies scratched their heads and then picked up their musical instruments and began playing, the imps started dancing once more and the elf butlers went back to serving the food. Soon everyone was enjoying themselves just as before.

"Look at King Merry!" said Summer.

The king was sitting on his throne, looking surprised and slightly dazed. He stretched and then stood up. He beamed happily as he looked down upon all of his guests, who were obviously having a wonderful time.

"He's forgotten too!" said Ellie in relief.

"There you are, girls," King Merry said as he walked over to them. "I was just wondering where...*RRRIBBIT!* Oh my goodness!" He put his hand up to his

mouth, looked
very surprised
at the noise
he'd just
made.

"Don't
worry,
King
Merry,"
Trixi said
hastily. "You've just got a nasty cough.
Come on, why don't we go and find you
some cough mixture?" She winked at the
girls and led him away.

"So, girls?" The girls looked up to see
Maybelle flying above their heads on
her leaf. "Why don't you come with
me? We need to talk where we won't be
overheard."

Summer, Jasmine and Ellie followed
Maybelle deep into the palace gardens.
They stopped near the beautiful
lemonade fountain, but for once the girls
were too worried to even think about
trying to catch the delicious sugary
bubbles that rose from it.

"I'll have to do some research to
find what ingredients we need for the
counter-potion," Maybelle told them.

"The only ingredient I know for sure that's in it is bubblebee honeycomb."

"Maybe we can look for the honeycomb while you work out what the other ingredients are," Ellie suggested. Summer and Jasmine nodded.

Just then Trixi zoomed out of the palace on her leaf. "I've given King Merry some cough syrup and left him back at the party," she said anxiously. "Have you worked out what we have to do for the potion?"

"First we've got to get some bubblebee honeycomb," Jasmine told her.

"Er, what exactly is bubblebee honeycomb, anyway?" Ellie asked.

"It's a very rare substance made only by the bubblebees," Maybelle explained. "It's the key to their bubblebee magic. And it's also a delicious treat, if you can find it!"

"But surely the bees will give us some honeycomb if it's going to help King Merry?" Summer asked.

"Yes, but first you'll have to find them," Maybelle told her. "They are some of the most mysterious creatures in the Secret Kingdom. They live deep in the jungle on Bubble Volcano, but no one knows exactly where their hive is. Clara Columbus, the famous imp explorer, is at Bubble Volcano at the moment. She's been searching for the hive all year long to ask the bees why there's less honeycomb." She rubbed her forehead. "If anyone knows where the hive is, it's Clara Columbus."

"So we'll find Clara, and then we'll find the bubblebees!" Summer exclaimed.

"Let's go!" Trixi said anxiously. "King Merry might have forgotten he's turning into a stink toad, but there's no time to lose!"

Flying High!

"We need to find Clara Columbus as fast as we can!" Jasmine cried.

"But how are we going to get ourselves to where she is?" Ellie asked.

"We can use King Merry's magic slide," Summer said, looking over at the rainbow slide, which disappeared into the depths of a pretty pond. It could take you to anywhere you wanted to go in the Secret Kingdom.

"Good idea, Summer!" Trixi said. "Do you remember how to use it? You just say where you want to go and then slide down into the pond."

Jasmine went first. "Take us to Clara Columbus at Bubble Volcano!" she cried as she whizzed down the rainbow. She didn't feel cold and wet as she hit the water. Instead she felt like she was being tossed and turned in a flurry of bright rainbow-coloured lights.

"Woohoo!' she called as she shot out the other side and landed in a large mound of foamy bubbles.

Seconds later, Summer appeared and then Ellie, and finally Trixi flew out on her leaf.

The girls climbed out of the bubbly pool and onto the rocks surrounding it.

They looked up to see that they were
in the middle of a jungle. Lush vines
hung from the branches and creepers
twined over everything. Big red, blue and
orange flowers bloomed everywhere and
they could hear the sound of a stream
gurgling nearby.

"Look at all the birds!" Summer gasped. Brightly coloured parrots and cockatoos swooped around overhead, their tails leaving streams of glitter in the air behind them.

"Clara must be here somewhere," Ellie said, looking around.

"Clara!" Jasmine shouted, making all the birds in the trees overhead take off in fright.

"CLARA!" Summer and Ellie joined in.

Suddenly there was a rusting in the undergrowth nearby. Summer, Ellie and Jasmine looked at one another anxiously, worried that they'd disturbed a dangerous jungle animal.

Then a voice called out from the trees. "Who's there?" it shouted.

"That's her!" Trixi cried, twirling round on her leaf in excitement. "Clara? It's Trixi. King Merry needs your help!"

"*My* help?" They heard the sound of someone striding through the trees. A curtain of vines was pushed aside and

then Clara Columbus appeared. She was
wearing long green socks, sturdy ankle
boots, camouflage shorts, a rucksack
and a jacket with lots of pockets. Her
long blonde hair was covered with an
explorer's hat. She put her hands on her
hips and stared at the
girls. "So what can
I do for you?" she
asked briskly.

"Clara, this is
Ellie, Summer
and Jasmine."
Trixi pointed
at each of the
girls in turn.

Clara shook
their hands. Her
jacket sleeve was torn,

and her hand was a bit muddy, but her smile was very kind.

"We really need your help, Clara," Jasmine said. "Something dreadful has happened."

Trixi explained everything that had gone on at the ball. "We have to cure King Merry," she finished. "And to do that we need to find some bubblebee honeycomb."

"I've been exploring Bubble Volcano for months, trying to find where the bubblebees live…" Clara told them.

The girls looked at each other in dismay.

"Luckily," Clara continued, "I finally found their hive this morning! I'll show you the way there and then we can ask the bubblebees for some honeycomb. But we must be careful. Bubblebees can be tricky creatures. Treat them with respect and politeness and they'll behave in the same way to you, but be rude and they'll get angry and attack. You don't want to feel one of their stings!"

"We'll be as polite as we can," said Summer.

"It's this way," Clara said as she strode away through the trees. "Come on!"

The girls grinned at one another and ran after her.

"So where exactly is the hive, Clara?" asked Trixi, flying alongside on her leaf.

Clara opened her mouth. "In the—"

GRRRRRRRR! A loud growl rumbled behind them, interrupting Clara.

They all swung around. Trixi gave a terrified squeak as an enormous black panther wearing plates of silver armour charged towards them through the trees, his lip curled back in a snarl, his ferocious teeth showing. On his back, perched on a silver throne, was a bony figure with a tuft of black frizzy hair.

"Oh, no!" gasped Summer. "Queen Malice!"

Bubblebee Hunt!

"Meddling humans!" snarled Queen Malice as the panther slunk closer, his long claws digging into the soft ground and his black eyes gleaming. "So you think you can make the counter-potion, do you?" She glared at them. "Even if you work out what ingredients you need, you'll never find them all – I'll make sure of that! You won't stop me from taking over the kingdom this time!"

Jasmine stepped forward, her chin lifted and her brown eyes flashing bravely. "Yes, we will!"

"Silence!" demanded Queen Malice.

"No," said Jasmine defiantly. "We're not like your Storm Sprites. You can't tell us what to do!"

"We won't let you turn King Merry into a stink toad," Ellie added.

"And everyone in the Secret Kingdom loves him," Summer declared, "so they'll all help us."

"That's right," Clara agreed. "Starting with me! I'm going to show these girls where the bubblebee honeycomb is, and you can't stop me!"

"That's what you think!" Queen Malice cackled. "You'll be no good to them at all once I've finished with you!" She lifted her hand and pointed it at Clara:

> "Be confused, forgetful, in a daze,
> All thoughts lost within a maze.
> Nothing will help you, no cure bring,
> Until you hear the queen bee sing."

There was a bright green flash and Queen Malice laughed loudly. "And you'll *never* hear the queen bee sing, because you won't be able to find her if you can't remember where the hive is!" she cried. The queen threw back her head and cackled. The panther joined in with a loud roar and then turned round and raced away through the jungle, with the queen laughing out loud as she urged it on.

"Clara!" Jasmine turned anxiously to the imp. "Are you all right?"

Clara looked at her in surprise. "Yes, fine, thank you!"

The girls breathed a sigh of relief as Clara smiled brightly at them. But their happiness faded as Clara spoke again.

"My name's…" Her voice trailed off and a look of surprise entered her eyes. "I can't remember!"

"You're Clara Columbus!" Summer cried. "The great imp explorer!"

"Me?" Clara asked.

"Yes," said Trixi, wringing her hands anxiously.

Clara giggled. "I'm not an explorer!" She skipped over to a nearby bank and started humming to herself and picking flowers. "I'm…well, I don't know what I am, but I'm certainly *not* an explorer!"

"Oh, no," said Summer in dismay. "She's forgotten *everything*!"

"Clara, you *are* an explorer," Ellie said

gently. "You said you found where the bubblebees lived and we need you to tell us where to find the hive."

Clara looked confused. "What are bubblebees?" she asked.

Trixi turned to the others. "What are we going to do?" she asked anxiously.

"Don't worry," Jasmine said practically. "Poor Clara might not be able to help us, but the bees must be around here somewhere. She said she found their hive this morning, so it can't be too far away."

"Exactly," Ellie agreed. "We'll just have to look around until we find them – even if we have to search the whole volcano."

Summer nodded. "We can't give up. King Merry is depending on us."

"Look at my lovely flowers," sang Clara as she skipped over with a bunch of purple and blue blooms. "I want to make a pretty bouquet."

Summer looked into Clara's eyes and tried to get her to focus. "Clara, can you remember anything about how to get to the bubblebee hive?" she asked.

"On top of the world!" Clara cried. "The whole world."

"It's like a riddle all over again!" Ellie sighed.

"Except we're not even sure she's leading us to the bubblebees," Jasmine said. "She's so confused that she doesn't know what she's saying."

Ellie heard a rustle behind them and looked round. "What was that?" she asked.

"I didn't hear anything," said Jasmine.

"There was a noise in the bushes," Ellie

said, walking over to investigate. She looked in all the shrubs but she didn't find anything.

"It's not Queen Malice again, is it?" Summer gasped. The girls looked round anxiously, but they couldn't see any sign of the queen or the panther.

"It was probably just an animal or a bird," said Trixi. "Don't worry about it."

"Pretty!" came a voice from over near the trees. Everyone turned to look at Clara, who had wandered off to pick more flowers.

"Poor Clara," said Summer sadly.

"She mentioned something about the top of the world," Ellie said thoughtfully. "Maybe she meant somewhere high?"

"Like the top of the volcano!" Jasmine cried, pointing up at the sky.

The girls looked up through the trees. Up in the clouds they could just see the top of a volcano. There were pretty silver bubbles spilling out of it that looked like shiny soapsuds.

"I think you might be right!" Ellie's cheeks flushed with excitement.

"It's so high it does look like the top of the world!" Summer breathed.

"Come on," Jasmine called as she headed off toward the volcano. "Let's go!"

Summer grabbed Clara's hand. "Come along, Clara," she said gently. "We've got to follow Jasmine!"

The girls stumbled and tripped through the lush undergrowth, climbing over fallen trees thick with green moss and pushing aside long creepers that hung down from overhead branches.

Parrots screeched and squawked as they flew overhead.

"Look!" exclaimed Jasmine as they came into a clearing and saw a beautiful bush covered with silver bubbles. She pointed at a strip of green fabric that was caught on a low branch.

Ellie bent down to pick it up.

"Clara's jacket!" Summer grinned. She took the material and held it up to the tear in the sleeve of Clara's coat. It fitted perfectly.

"Clara's been this way before," said Ellie. "We're on the right track!"

"The bubblebee hive *must* be at the top of the volcano!" Trixi said gleefully.

"Hee, hee, hee!" came a voice from behind the trees. "Thanks for the tip!"

The girls all gasped as a grey pointed
face popped out from behind a nearby
bush.

"It's a Storm Sprite!" exclaimed
Jasmine, looking at the creature's bat-like
wings and spiky hair.

"Not just one," Ellie
said in horror as
four more sprites
jumped out from
their hiding
places around
the girls. Their
eyes glittered
and they cackled
with glee. "Look at
them all!" she cried. "They must have
been spying on us!"

"We have!" the leader of the sprites

laughed. "And you've led us straight to the bubblebees!"

"We're going to take all the honeycomb so there'll be none left for you!" crowed another sprite. "Queen Malice will be so pleased with us!" He flapped his wings and took off into the sky.

"And soon King Merry will be a toad," a third cried nastily.

"RIBBIT, RIBBIT!" the sprites all taunted meanly as they rose into the air and flew away up through the trees.

"Quick!" Trixi gasped. "We have to find the bubblebee hive before they do!"

Bubblebees

It was a race to the top of the volcano!
As the sprites flapped overhead, Jasmine,
Ellie, Summer and Clara pushed their
way through the undergrowth and
dodged round bushes and rocks. Trixi
zoomed along beside them, ducking
under hanging vines and round tree
branches, with Clara running closely
behind.

Finally the girls burst out of the trees into a clearing right at the top of the volcano. They could see the round hole of the crater in front of them. There were thousands of bubbles floating out of it, and buzzing between them were lots of big fluffy bubblebees!

The bubblebees were nothing like the bees that the girls had in their gardens back at home in the Other Realm. They were much larger for a start – about the size of guinea pigs – and instead of being yellow and black, their fluffy coats were dark pink and lilac. They buzzed along merrily as they zipped in and out between the bubbles and landed on the flowers that decorated the volcano slopes.

"Look at them all!" said Summer. "They're *so* cute!"

"I can't see their hive, though," said Jasmine, looking round frantically. "We've got to find it before the Storm Sprites get here!"

"Hello, little bees," called Clara, making a soft buzzing noise. "Can we *bee* friends?"

"Clara, can you tell me where the hive is?" Summer asked, but Clara didn't answer. She was too busy giggling as a bee came over and buzzed in front of her nose.

"Oh, no!" Jasmine cried suddenly, pointing up at the sky. "They're here!"

Sure enough, four Storm Sprites were flying down towards them. The bees swarmed around them curiously, but the sprites shooed them away with their bony fingers.

"Get out of our way!" yelled one of the sprites.

"Yeah, move it, you fluffy freaks!" snapped the sprite next to him. "We want to land!"

But the bees took no notice. More of them came over and they all just buzzed round the sprites curiously.

"Come on, you useless lot!" the leader yelled to the other sprites. "We have to find that hive for Queen Malice. Squash the bees if you need to!"

"No!" Summer gasped as the sprites started bumping into the poor bees and swatting them out of the air. The bees started buzzing louder and flying faster, trying to get away from the horrible sprites.

"Stop it!" Summer yelled at the sprites. She didn't usually lose her temper, but she couldn't bear to see any animal being hurt. "Get away from them!"

"Or what?" jeered the sprite leader. He gave a cackle and then swiped at another bubblebee, who swerved and flew down into the volcano crater, out of reach of the sprite's pointy fingers.

As Summer watched the little bee fly down into the opening, she remembered something Clara had said earlier – something about the whole world. *Maybe she didn't mean whole*, Summer thought as she peered into the gaping mouth of the crater, *maybe she meant hole*. Summer looked down, and as her eyes got used to the darkness she spotted a glimmer of gold peeking out near one of the walls...

Summer turned to call Ellie and
Jasmine, but as she did so a Storm
Sprite swiped at a bubblebee, knocking
it straight at her! Summer reached out
to catch it, and as she grabbed the bee
she was knocked off balance. Her arms
whirled around as she fell backwards —
and tumbled down into the volcano!

Ellie screamed as her friend
disappeared.

"Summer!" shouted Jasmine.

Trixi turned pale. They all rushed to the crater's edge, their hearts pounding as they peered down into the gloom below.

"I'm okay!" came a shout.

Ellie and Jasmine sighed in relief. As their eyes adjusted to the dark, they could just make out a ledge of rock on the inside of the crater. Summer was sitting on it, holding the little bubblebee, who had an injured leg.

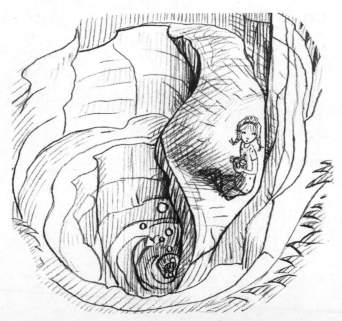

"More than okay!" Summer looked up at them, her eyes shining. "Look!" She pointed at the wall in front of her. There, built into the side of the volcano, was a beautiful golden hive! It was as tall as Summer and had walls made of shining hexagonal cells all joined together with honey. There were six golden turrets on the sides and an open hexagon in the middle that bees were buzzing in and out of.

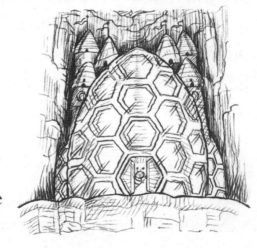

"I've found the bubblebee hive!" said Summer with a grin.

Jasmine and Ellie quickly began climbing down to the ledge and Trixi zoomed down behind them. Clara carefully placed her bouquet of flowers in her backpack and followed the others down onto the ledge.

"Let's go in!" said Jasmine eagerly as they stared at the enormous hive.

"They've found the hive!" crowed a voice from above them.

The girls looked at one another in horror as the sprites started to flap down to the ledge.

"What are we going to do?" wailed Trixi. "We have to stop them!"

Suddenly the injured bee flew out of Summer's arms and over to the other bubblebees that were buzzing round the hive. He hovered in front of them and then started to move in a funny zigzagging dance. All the bees stopped to watch as he flew to the left and the right and up and down, buzzing all the way.

"What's he doing?" asked Ellie.

"I think that's how they talk!" said Summer. "Bees in our world talk by dancing and waggling. Maybe it's the same here?"

"Oh, yes!" Trixi said. "I think I remember reading something Clara wrote about bubblebee dance conversations."

"I wonder what he's saying," said Jasmine.

The bee turned and pointed his stinger at the Storm Sprites. Suddenly all the bees turned to look at the sprites. Their merry buzzing became loud and fierce and their stingers quivered.

"I think he's telling them about how he was injured!" said Ellie.

"It was the sprites!" Jasmine cried, pointing to the Storm Sprites and hoping the bees understood. "They're after your honeycomb. Get them!"

The bees buzzed furiously and swarmed towards the sprites.

"What are they doing?" one of the sprites called nervously as the bees buzzed closer.

Another one tried to hit a bubblebee out of the air. The buzzing got louder and the bees suddenly attacked the Storm Sprites, stinging them all over.

"Ow! Ohh! Ow!" the Storm Sprites yelled.

"I'm getting out of here!" yelled the sprite leader, flying away as fast as his

 leathery wings could carry him.

The others followed. They flew up to the clouds, so high that they looked like black specks, and then vanished completely.

"Hooray!" exclaimed Jasmine. "Well done, becs!"

The girls hugged one another in delight.

The injured bee flew back over and buzzed up and down in front of them.

"I think he's trying to tell us something," Summer said. "He keeps going over to the door of the hive. Maybe he's inviting us in?"

"What if he's not?" Ellie wondered. "If

we enter their hive without permission, the bubblebees could attack us too!"

"If only there were some way to understand them," Jasmine sighed.

"The magical unicorn horn!" Summer gasped. "It lets us talk to animals!"

Suddenly there was a tinkling noise and the Magic Box appeared on the ledge in front of them. The lid opened, displaying the six magical gifts inside.

Ellie took out the tiny silver horn. As soon as she had it in her hand, the lid of the Magic Box closed, and with a tiny *pop*, the whole box disappeared. "Let's talk to the bees and see if it's okay for us to go into the hive," Ellie said.

"And ask them for some bubblebee honeycomb for King Merry!" added Summer.

Ellie held the unicorn horn tightly in her hand. She could still hear the injured bee buzzing around, but now she could understand what his dance meant.

"Thank you for helping me," he was saying. "Please come into the hive and meet my queen."

Ellie tried to say thank you, but instead she found herself doing a little hop backwards and wiggling to the left. She was talking to him in bubblebee dance! "That would be wonderful," she told him with another few steps.

Summer and Jasmine giggled when they saw Ellie zigzagging about just like a bubblebee.

"He wants us to go inside and meet the queen," Ellie translated.

"I'll make you small enough to go

in," Trixi said. She tapped her ring and
chanted:

*"So you can enter the hive with me,
Shrink to the size of a bubblebee!"*

Suddenly the girls found themselves
getting smaller and smaller until the
hive loomed over them. They followed
the bubblebee as he flew through the
hexagon door. Inside the hive, the walls
were all covered with golden honey and
a delicious scent wafted through the air.

"This way!" the bubblebee danced.
"The queen is in her courtroom."

The bee led them down several twisty
narrow corridors into a small hexagonal
room.

At one end of the room there was a

small golden throne with an enormous
bee sitting on it. On her head was a tiny
crown edged with hexagons. She buzzed
in surprise when she saw the girls.

The injured bee started to dance in front
of her. "I have brought some visitors, Your
Majesty," he told the queen.

"He's telling her all about us and the
Storm Sprites," Ellie explained to the
others as they watched the little bee twirl
and bounce in front of the queen.

When the bee finished, the queen

turned her big eyes on the girls and fluttered off her throne. She began to dance. "This bee tells me you saved him," she said. "I am very grateful."

"You should talk for all of us, Jasmine," Ellie told her after she'd translated the queen's moves. "You're the best at dancing!" She handed Jasmine the unicorn horn.

"Your Majesty," Jasmine began, waggling from side to side. "We came here to ask for your help. King Merry is in trouble."

"King Merry?" echoed the queen.

In a few steps Jasmine explained everything that had happened. "We really need some bubblebee honeycomb for the counter-potion," she finished with a twirl.

"I'd love to give you some," the queen

danced back. "But we only have one piece left, and we need it to keep our bee magic alive." She held up a glass jar with a small piece of honeycomb inside. This honeycomb looked different than the golden honey in the rest of the hive. It was a darker gold colour and it had little purple and blue flecks in it, like bits of flower petals. The honeycomb glowed faintly for a moment and then faded out.

"We haven't been able to make any new honeycomb lately," the queen explained. "It can only be made using honeyflowers and blossoms from mountain cherry trees. There used to be honeyflowers all over Bubble Volcano, but every year we find fewer and fewer. This year we couldn't find any." She sighed.

"Isn't there anything we can do?"

Jasmine asked with a hop and a shuffle.

"I wish we could help," the queen
replied. "But we unless
we get some more
honeyflowers,
we can't make
any more
honeycomb."

Jasmine
translated for
the others.

"Oh, no!"
Trixi cried.
"What are we
going to do? We
can't let King Merry
turn into a stink toad!"

"I guess we're just going to have to
find some honeyflowers!" Jasmine said

determinedly. "There have to be some growing somewhere."

"We'll just have to search the whole volcano until we find them," Ellie agreed.

"What do they look like?" Jasmine asked the queen bee.

"Honeyflowers are blue with pointed petals covered in tiny purple spots," the queen buzzed. "They usually grow near lakes and riverbanks."

Jasmine translated for the others. "If the honeyflowers grow near the water, then that's where we'll start," she said as she raced toward the door. "Come on! There's no time to lose!"

A Problem Solved!

"Hang on," Ellie said suddenly, stopping Jasmine in her tracks. "What did the queen say the honeyflowers looked like?"

"Blue flowers with purple spots," Summer reminded her.

"And they grow near *riverbanks*?" Ellie asked.

"Yes," said Jasmine. "Why?"

Ellie rushed over to Clara and started rummaging in the explorer's rucksack. "Blue flowers with purple spots..." she muttered to herself. "I knew it!" she suddenly shouted, pulling Clara's flowers out of her bag and holding them up for everyone to see. "Look! Some of them are blue with purple spots! And Clara picked them near the riverbank at the bottom of the volcano!"

"Brilliant!" said Jasmine. "Let's ask the queen if these are the right flowers." She handed Ellie the unicorn horn.

"Are *these* honeyflowers, Your Majesty?" Ellie danced,

holding out the flowers for her to see.

The girls didn't need to be holding the unicorn horn to understand the queen bee's delighted response. She got up from her throne and danced a happy little jig before taking the flowers from Ellie.

But then suddenly Clara pounced toward the queen and snatched the flowers back. "Mine!" she declared. "Pretty!"

"She's very confused," Ellie explained to the queen. "Queen Malice put a spell on her so that she couldn't show us the way to your hive."

"Oh!" Summer cried, her eyes shining. "But you can fix it! Don't you remember, Ellie? Queen Malice said Clara would be confused until she heard the queen bee sing."

"That's right!" Ellie breathed. "Would you sing for Clara, Your Majesty? Then I'm sure she'll let us give you the honeyflowers."

The queen bee smiled and nodded happily.

Ellie handed the unicorn horn to Clara, and then she, Jasmine, Summer and Trixi all placed a finger on it so they'd be able to hear the queen's song too.

The queen flew over to Clara and circled round her. Then she held up the jar with the honeycomb in it and started to sing in a beautiful high voice.

*"With honeyflowers and mountain cherry,
We'll make honeycomb for King Merry."*

The honeycomb glowed brighter and

brighter as the queen sang. The golden
light washed over Clara.

After the queen's song ended, Clara
clutched her head. She blinked several
times and looked around. "Goodness, I
feel strange!" she said dazedly. "Is this
a dream? Am I really in the bubblebee
hive?"

"Queen Malice's spell is wearing off!"
exclaimed Ellie.

"Yes, you're really in the bubblebee

hive," Jasmine told Clara. "Queen Malice put a spell on you so you'd be too confused to show us where the hive was. But we managed to find it anyway."

"Thanks to our new bubblebee friend," Summer said, patting the little injured bubblebee's fluffy pink and purple coat.

"And this is the queen bee," Jasmine said, pointing over at where the queen was sitting on her throne.

Clara gasped and gave a deep curtsey.

"She needs the honeyflowers you picked to make bubblebee honeycomb for the counter-potion to cure King Merry," Trixi explained.

"You'll give them to her, won't you, Clara?" Summer asked.

"Yes, of course!" Clara held the flowers up to the queen, still holding the unicorn horn in her other hand. "You can have as many as you like, Your Majesty."

The queen buzzed in delight. "That would be wonderful," she danced happily.

"I can't believe I'm actually in the bubblebees' hive!" Clara said, looking around. "This is amazing!" She bowed to the queen and danced a few delicate steps. "It's an honour to meet you, Your Majesty," she said. "I've been searching for you for a long time. I've always dreamed of studying you and your hive up close."

"Would you like to stay with us for a while?" asked the queen.

"Oh, yes!" said Clara excitedly. "And I'll show you where I found the honeyflowers. There are lots of them growing near the riverbank at the bottom of the volcano!"

The queen flew over to Summer, handed her the jar with the piece of honeycomb inside and started to dance. Clara held the unicorn horn out for Trixi and the girls to touch so they could all hear what the queen was saying.

"You can use this for King Merry's counter-potion," the queen told them. "With the flowers Clara found, we'll be able to make enough honeycomb to keep our bubblebee magic alive for a long time."

Trixi curtseyed on her leaf. "Thank you so much."

"And there's enough extra honeycomb in there for you each to try a small piece, if you'd like," the queen said.

"Oh, yes please!" they all said excitedly.

Summer reached into the jar, broke off enough tiny pieces of honeycomb for everyone and handed them out.

As Ellie bit into her piece of honeycomb, she felt it explode into her mouth, tasting of toffee and honey. It was one of the most delicious things that she had ever eaten. "Yum!" she breathed.

"It's delicious!" agreed Jasmine.

"Wow!" said Trixi, doing a little spin on her leaf.

Jasmine led the others in a bubblebee

dance thank-you. They
all jumped back and
wiggled to the left.

"You're very
welcome," the
queen buzzed.
"I just hope
you have as
much luck
finding the rest
of the ingredients
you need."

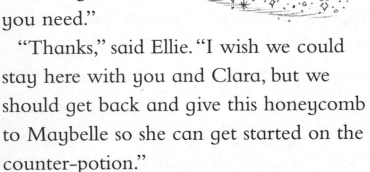

"Thanks," said Ellie. "I wish we could
stay here with you and Clara, but we
should get back and give this honeycomb
to Maybelle so she can get started on the
counter-potion."

"Can you magic us back to the
Enchanted Palace, Trixi?" Jasmine asked.

"Of course," Trixi said. She tapped her ring and chanted:

"Good friends fly to stop the curse,
Before King Merry gets much worse."

"Goodbye!" Jasmine, Summer and Ellie called to their new friends as a bright purple flash surrounded them. They closed their eyes as they began spinning round in a whirlwind. When they opened them again, they had landed back in the palace ballroom.

The party was still in full swing. The elves and pixies were still dancing and Maybelle was hovering beside King Merry while he sat on his throne.

"I just don't understand why I have such a bad cough," they heard him

tell her. "I wish it would go away…
RIBBIT!"

"There, there," Maybelle soothed. "It
will soon be gone.
Why don't you
go and dance
and enjoy
the party?"

King
Merry went
over to the
dance floor,
but instead of
dancing he started
hopping up and down like a toad!

"Oh dear," said Ellie. "We really need
to find the other five ingredients as fast
as we can!" Summer and Jasmine nodded
nervously.

Maybelle came flying over to them on her leaf.

"We got the bubblebee honeycomb, Aunt Maybelle!" said Trixi.

"Wonderful!" her aunt said in relief. "I'll consult my books and find out what the next ingredient is."

"As soon as Maybelle finds out what we need, I'll send you a message in the Magic Box," Trixi told the girls. "But for now, we'd better say goodbye."

Trixi kissed each of them on the nose and then conjured up a whirlwind. It swirled around the girls, spinning them round and round in a cloud of golden sparkles and carrying them back to Ellie's bedroom. They landed on the rug on her bedroom floor. The Magic Box sat on the floor between them.

"Oh, wow," breathed Jasmine. "What an adventure that was!"

Ellie nodded. "I can't wait until we go back! I wonder what ingredient we'll have to find next time..."

"And where in the Secret Kingdom we'll have to go to look for it," Summer added.

"Wherever it is, I want to go back soon and help poor King Merry," Jasmine said.

A ripple ran across the mirror in the Magic Box. The girls exchanged excited looks. This adventure might be over, but another was just around the corner!

In the next Secret Kingdom adventure, Ellie, Summer and Jasmine visit

Sugarsweet Bakery

Read on for a sneak peek...

A New Adventure!

It was a beautiful summer's day. The blue sky was dotted with fluffy clouds and the sun was shining down on Honeyvale Park, which was filled with people walking their dogs and feeding the ducks. Over by the oak trees, Summer Hammond's mum was setting out a birthday tea for one of Summer's little brothers, Finn.

"Isn't it lovely today?" Summer asked her two best friends, Jasmine Smith and Ellie Macdonald.

Jasmine nodded, her dark ponytail bouncing up and down. "It's the perfect afternoon for a birthday picnic!"

"Let's go and see the ducks," Summer suggested.

"Wait," Ellie said. "Your mum's calling us." She pointed over to where Mrs Hammond was waving to them from a sea of colourful picnic blankets.

The girls ran over to see what she wanted.

"Girls, could you do me a favour please?" Mrs Hammond asked. "I need some help with one of the party games. Can you hide these stars before Finn and his friends arrive? Then, when they get here, they can all try and find them." She took a bag of silver cardboard stars from one of the picnic hampers.

"No problem, Mum," said Summer.

"Don't go too far away, and don't hide any too close to the duck pond — we don't want anyone falling in!" Mrs Hammond said with a smile.

The girls took the bag and set off around the park.

"Okay, let's split the stars up and each hide some," Jasmine said, handing handfuls of stars to Ellie and Summer.

The three girls ran off in separate directions, hiding stars in bushes and in hollowed-out tree trunks, on benches and near the edges of flowerbeds. Finally there was just one star left. Summer held it up. "Where shall I hide this?" she asked as Ellie and Jasmine walked back over to her.

"How about beside that bench by the pond?" suggested Ellie. "It's not too close to the water."

They all ran over. Jasmine moved some of the long grass and bent down to hide the star by the leg of the bench. But as she did so, there was a loud croak and a toad jumped out! Jasmine squealed and leaped back.

Ellie laughed. "Jasmine, it's only a toad!"

"I know, but it gave me a fright!" Jasmine giggled.

"Poor thing," Summer said, watching the little creature hop away. "I bet it was more scared of you, Jasmine!"

She watched the toad sadly as it

hopped away. It had reminded her
of their friend, King Merry. He was
the ruler of an amazing place called
the Secret Kingdom, which the girls
had discovered when they'd brought
a beautifully carved box home from
their school jumble sale. The box had
summoned them to the Secret Kingdom
so that they could help undo the trouble
that King Merry's awful sister, Queen
Malice, had caused when everyone in the
kingdom had decided that they wanted
King Merry to rule instead of her. With
the help of their pixie friend, Trixi, the
girls had managed to break Queen
Malice's spell and save the kingdom,
but now the queen had done something
even worse – she'd poisoned King Merry
with a terrible curse that was slowly

transforming him into a stink toad!

"I do hope poor King Merry is okay," Summer said anxiously.

"Do you think he's starting to look like a toad?" Jasmine asked.

"Oh, I hope not," said Ellie. "If only we knew what the next ingredient in the counter-potion was!"

The girls knew that the only chance of curing King Merry was to make a special counter-potion from six rare ingredients. Jasmine, Summer and Ellie had already found the first ingredient, bubblebee honeycomb, but there were still five more ingredients left for them to get.

"Queen Malice is so mean," said Jasmine angrily. "I can't believe she's turning her own brother into a toad, all because she wants to rule the Secret Kingdom."

"I'd never do that to my brothers!" said Summer.

Jasmine pretended to look shocked. "Even after that time Finn put worms in your bed?"

"Well…" Summer grinned. "Maybe I'd turn him into a fluffy bunny, but not a stink toad!"

"Suuum-mer!" Mrs Hammond called. "Finn's here!"

Summer gazed over to the stand of oak trees to see Finn arriving with his friends. She pushed thoughts of the Secret Kingdom to the back of her mind. "Come on!" she said to Ellie and Jasmine. "It looks like the party's about to start!"

Finn and his friends had a great time

at the party. They played pass the parcel and musical statues and then went on a hunt for the silver stars. "Don't go out of sight!" Mrs Hammond called as the boys raced away.

"Don't worry, Mum," Summer said. "We'll keep an eye on them!"

Jasmine, Summer and Ellie ran after the boys and made sure they didn't go too far away.

Read
Sugarsweet Bakery
to find out what happens next!

Secret Kingdom

Enjoy six sparkling adventures.
Collect them all!

Out now!

Secret Kingdom

A magical world of friendship and fun!

Join best friends
Ellie, Summer and Jasmine at

www.secretkingdombooks.com

and enjoy games, sneak peeks
and lots more!

You'll find great activities, competitions, stories
and games, plus a special newsletter for
Secret Kingdom friends!

Secret Kingdom Codebreaker

Sssh! Can you keep a secret? Ellie, Summer and Jasmine have written a new special message just for you! They have written one secret word of their special message in each of the six Secret Kingdom books in series two. To discover the secret word, hold a small mirror to this page and see your word magically appear!

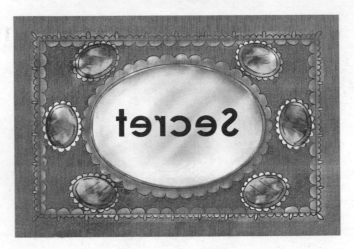

The first secret word is: _____

When you have cracked the code and found all six secret words,
work out the special message and go online to enter the competition at

www.secretkingdombooks.com

We will put all of the correct entries into a draw and select one winner to receive a special
Secret Kingdom goody bag featuring lots of sparkly gifts, including a glittery t-shirt!

You can also send your entry on a postcard to:

Secret Kingdom Competition, Orchard Books, 338 Euston Road, London, NW1 3BH

Don't forget to include your name and address.

Good luck!

Closing Date: 31st July 2013.

Collect the tokens from each Secret Kingdom book to get special Secret Kingdom gifts!

In every Secret Kingdom book there are three Friendship Tokens, that you can exchange for special gifts! Send your friendship tokens in to us as soon as you get them or save them up to get an even more special gift!

3 tokens

Secret Kingdom poster and collectable glittery bookmark

6 tokens

Scrummy scented stickers

8 tokens

Secret Kingdom pen

15 tokens

Glittery t-shirt

18 tokens

Secret Kingdom pink cap

To take part in this offer, please send us a letter telling us why you like Secret Kingdom. Don't forget to:
1) Tell us which gift you would like to exchange your tokens for
2) Include the correct number of Friendship Tokens for each gift you are requesting
3) Include your name and address
4) Include the signature of a parent or guardian

Secret Kingdom Friendship Token Offer
Orchard Books Marketing Department
338 Euston Road, London, NW1 3BH

Closing date: 31st May 2013

www.secretkingdombooks.com

1 Friendship Token
www.secretkingdombooks.com

1 Friendship Token
www.secretkingdombooks.com

1 Friendship Token
www.secretkingdombooks.com

Secret Kingdom

Look out for the next sparkling summer special!

Available
June 2013